this book belongs to:

_____

_____

D1090499

...is for Gecko

an alphabet adventure
in Hawai'i

BeachHouse

illustrated by Don Robinson

Illustrations by Don Robinson
Text and design by Jane Gillespie

ISBN-10: 1-933067-18-7
ISBN-13: 978-1-933067-18-6

First Printing, October 2006

BeachHouse Publishing, LLC
PO Box 2926
'Ewa Beach, Hawai'i 96706
email: info@beachhousepublishing.com
www.beachhousepublishing.com

Printed in Korea

is for the Auntie that shoos him away.

B is for the Broom she swings with dismay.

is for the **Cat**
that chases him
about.

is for the Door
that locks Meow
out.

E is for Early on a bright Hawaiian day.

F is for the **Flower** he smells on his way.

G is for **Gecko** strolling down the street.

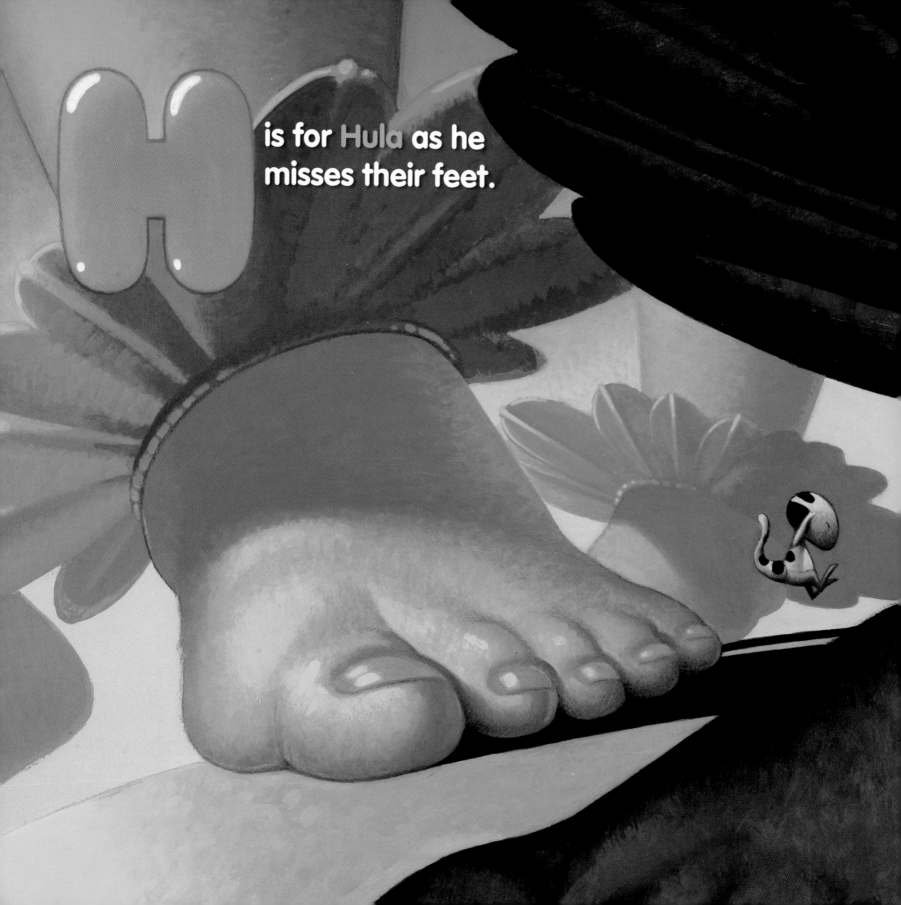

is for Ice making everything wet.

is for Jump as far as he can get.

is for **Kick** as he flies through the air.

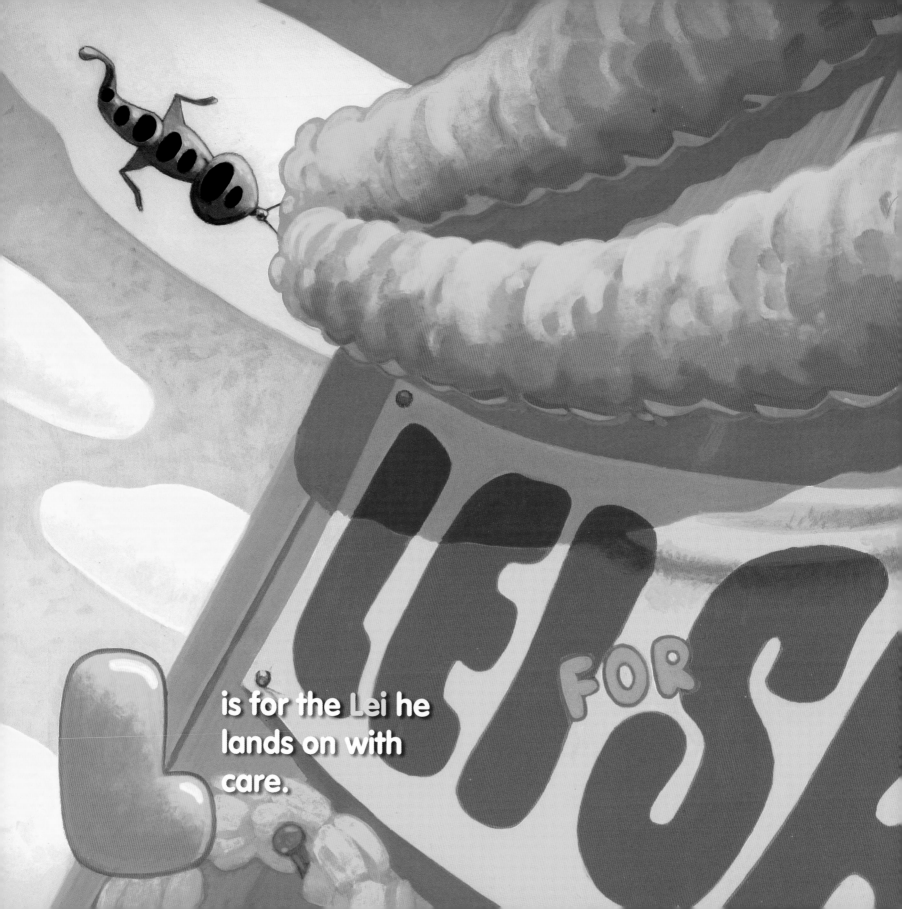

is for the Lei he lands on with care.

is for the Nēnē
waving goodbye.

is for the Quilt spread out on the grass.

is for the Runner he allows to pass.

S is for the Surf
slipping onto
the shore.

is for the Turtle
starting to snore.

is for Under the coconut tree.

is for Visit with friends by the sea.

is for **Walking**
alongside the
park.

X is for eXit before it gets dark.

is for his Yellow
step peeking
through a gap.

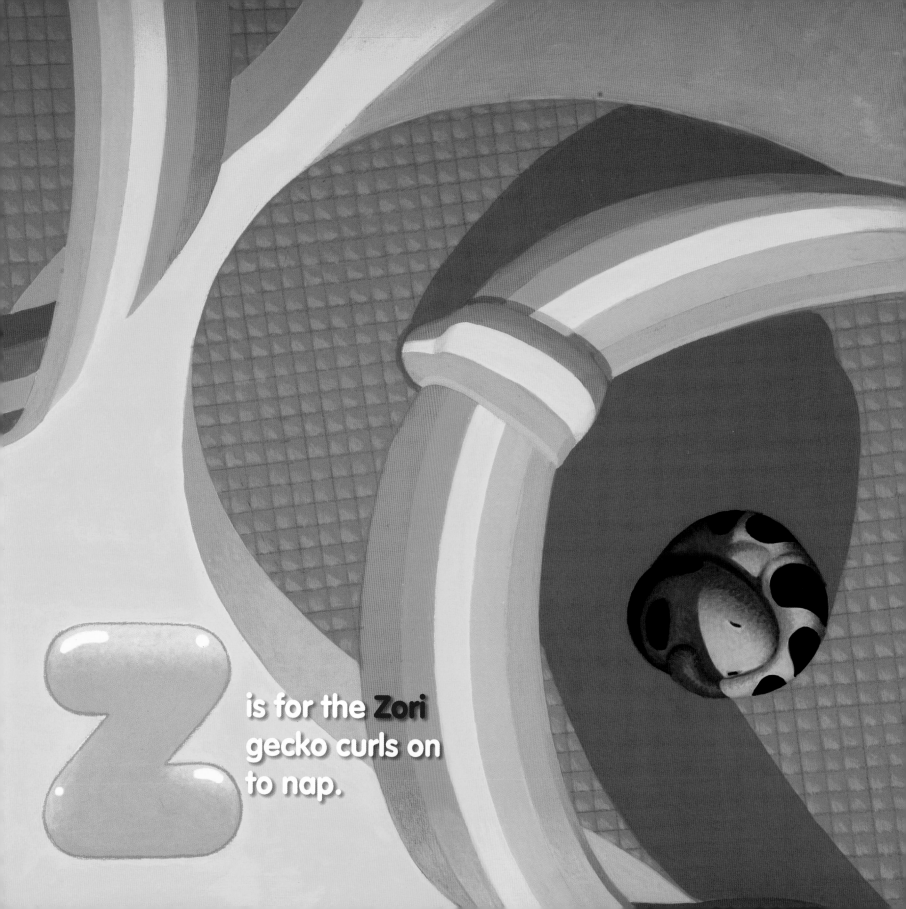

is for the **Zori** gecko curls on to nap.